This book belongs to:

To read with:

For Sidney – C.H.

For Laura and Sam – M.C.

RED SQUIRREL BOOKS

Published in 2014 in Great Britain by Barrington Stoke Ltd
18 Walker Street, Edinburgh, EH3 7LP

www.redsquirrelbooks.co.uk

This story was first published in a different form in *Wow! 366*, Scholastic Children's Books, 2008

Text © 2008 Charlie Higson
Illustrations © Mark Chambers

A CIP catalogue record for this book is available from the British Library upon request

ISBN 978-1-78112-373-7

Printed in China by Toppan Leefung PTE. Ltd

CHARLIE HIGSON   MARK CHAMBERS

Freddy and the PiG

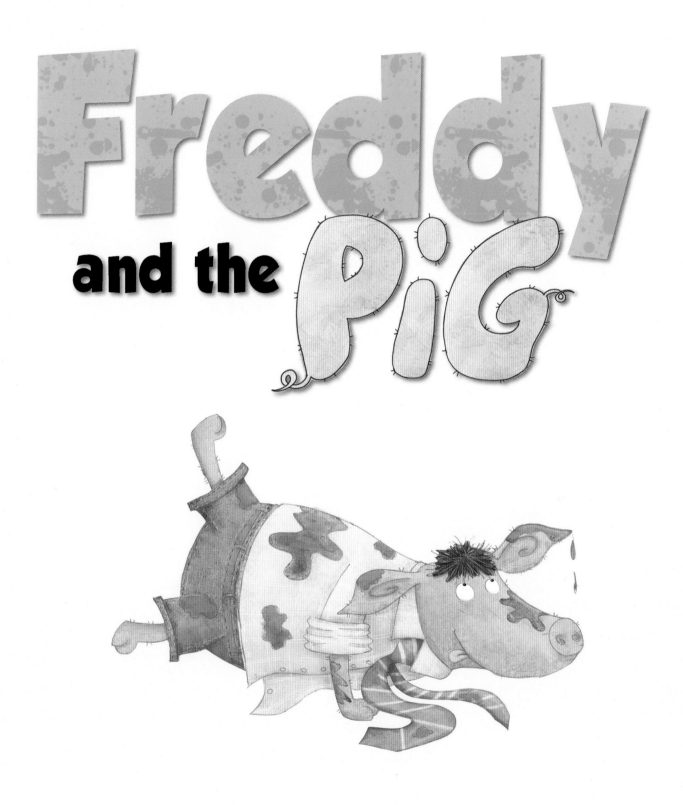

RED SQUIRREL BOOKS

Freddy hated school.

"It's boring and a waste of time," he told his teachers. "I'm going to spend the rest of my life playing Xbox, so why do I need to learn all this rubbish?"

One day he hit on a clever plan and sent a pig to school in his place. He dressed it in his school uniform and gave it an old pair of his glasses.

Freddy was not a thin boy, so the uniform fitted rather well.

The pig was very happy at school. It sat in class and it grunted. That was more than Freddy had ever done.

The teacher was very pleased with him. But when she handed out worksheets, the pig ate his and did a wee on the floor.

At home, Freddy ate everything in the fridge and sat on the floor all day playing his favourite Xbox game – Total Death War.

He was very happy.

When the pig came home at the end of the day,

he seemed happy too.

The next day Freddy sent the pig in again. The pig rolled in a puddle all morning.

But in the afternoon he got full marks in a maths test,
so nobody minded.

In fact, the pig enjoyed himself more and more each day he went in. Soon he was sticking his trotter up in class.

He even joined the football team.

In his first match he scored two goals and ate the ball at half-time. He was in heaven.

Freddy was in heaven too. He got to "Top Gun" level on Total Death War.

The only problem was that Freddy's mum couldn't tell Freddy and the pig apart any more.

Freddy had grown very fat and round, his arms and legs had shrunk from lack of use and he could only talk in grunts.

The pig seemed cleverer and he was more helpful around the house.

So in the end, Freddy's mum sold Freddy to a local farm and sent the pig to university, where he did Mud Studies.

The pig went on to set up his own very successful mud pie business, and even got elected as an MP.

In the end, Freddy was adopted by a family of vegetarians.

But they never let him in the house.